THE HISTORY CHANNEL® PRESENTS

HISTORY'S MYSTERIES®

The DEAD, the DOOMED, and the BURIED

Read all the books in

THE HISTORY CHANNEL® PRESENTS HISTORY'S MYSTERIES®

The DEAD, the DOOMED, and the BURIED

By Jane B. Mason and Sarah Hines Stephens

SCHOLASTIC INC.

New York   Toronto   London   Auckland   Sydney
Mexico City   New Delhi   Hong Kong   Buenos Aires

No part of this work may be reproduced, in whole or in
part, stored in a retrieval system, or transmitted in any
form or by any means, electronic, mechanical,
photocopying, recording, or otherwise, without
written permission of the publisher. For information
regarding permission, write to Scholastic Inc.,
Attention: Permissions Department, 557 Broadway, New
York, NY 10012.

ISBN 0-439-55706-2

The History Channel, the "H" logo and HISTORY'S
MYSTERIES are registered trademarks of A&E
Television Networks. © 2003 A&E
Television Networks. All Rights Reserved.

Published by Scholastic Inc.
SCHOLASTIC and associated logos are trademarks
and/or registered trademarks of Scholastic Inc.

12 11 10 9 8 7 6   4 5 6 7 8/0

Printed in the U.S.A.
First printing, September 2003

Visit Scholastic.com for information about our books
and authors online!

CONTENTS

CURSES!

Do you believe in lucky stars? What about *unlucky* stars? Some people, places, and things just seem to be doomed from the very beginning, while others are cursed at the bitter end. . . .

But what exactly does it mean to be doomed? Is it deserved? Do people and places earn a curse because of their own evil acts? Or are the cursed simply victims of unlucky circumstances?

There are many theories about how bad luck works. One old saying tells us that bad luck comes in threes. That adage seems to hold true for one famously doomed fleet — the *Titanic,* as well as her two sister ships, the *Britannic* and the *Olympic.* All three ships were involved in mysterious tragedies. Was it coincidence, or did they all set sail on an ill path?

If ships can be doomed, then what about places? One famous, spooky tower in London was home to so much death and unhappiness it became known as the "Bloody Tower"! Was the building cursed, or was it simply a spot that saw more than its share of torture, tragedy, and death?

Besides boats and buildings, people can be doomed, too — and not just the living! Many who have been lucky in life have terrible luck after they die. Their bodies might be stolen, or their tombs might be robbed. What motivates such ghoulish activities? Is it money, curiosity, or something more mysterious and sinister?

Read on and you will unearth new and ancient knowledge about doomed people and places throughout history. Together with The History Channel®, we have delved into the depths, dug into the dirt, and dredged up the details of the dead, the doomed, and the buried. . . .

TITANIC TRAGEDIES:
THREE DOOMED SISTER SHIPS

Almost everyone has heard about the sinking of the *Titanic* — it's probably the most famous ship disaster in history! But did you know the *Titanic* had two sister ships? They were called the *Britannic* and the *Olympic*, and they completed a trio of luxury ocean liners. These ships looked remarkably like the *Titanic* and they had similarly tragic fates.

THE BIRTH OF THE LUXURY LINER

In 1910, great ocean liners ruled the seas. A steady flow of immigrants filled the boats that crossed the ocean from Europe to North America. Ship owners, anxious to make money, built bigger ships to hold more passengers. But for most immigrants the voyage from the Old World to the new was a one-way, once-in-a-lifetime trip.

Looking for steadier business, ocean liner companies built new boats for new types of customers — wealthy, first-class travelers who made regular transatlantic trips for business and pleasure.

The bigger, faster, and more lavish ships attracted the rich and famous. And the rich and famous passengers drew attention to the stars of the seas — the great luxury liners.

FIERCE COMPETITION

In the early 1900s, two steamship lines, Cunard and White Star, competed fiercely for the wealthiest passengers. In 1907, Cunard introduced the *Lusitania*. She was the newest, largest, most decked-out ship on the ocean. Until the *Lusitania* was launched, White Star had owned the most luxurious ships. But next to the *Lusitania* their fleet looked pretty shabby!

White Star immediately began designing three even bigger and more luxurious ships. The new ships were called "Olympic class." They weighed forty-five thousand tons each and were by far the largest in the world.

The first two White Star ships, the *Titanic* and

SUNKEN TREASURE

The names that the White Star chairman originally chose for his three new ships were: *Olympic*, *Titanic*, and *Gigantic*. All three names come from Greek mythology and they all mean "huge"!

the *Olympic*, were built side by side in a shipyard in Belfast, Ireland. It was the first time that two giant ships were built at the same time in the same yard. Getting them done on schedule was a huge challenge!

OLYMPIC LAUNCH

The *Olympic* was completed and launched on October 20, 1910. A crowd of thousands gathered at the dock to watch.

At the crowded launch, a twenty-three-year-old woman fought her way on board. Her name was Violet Jessop, and she was set to work as a steward on the *Olympic*. Like the rest of the crew, Violet was impressed by the ship's luxury. But the young steward had no idea that she had just begun a long and strange relationship with the *Olympic* — and her two sister ships!

OLYMPIC OPULENCE

More than one hundred feet longer than any other ship, the *Olympic* was so big she made the

Lusitania look like a bathtub toy. The *Olympic* also offered extravagant comforts to her passengers. Luxuries included a gymnasium, Turkish baths, palm courts, and Parisian-style cafes. Every detail was ornate, right down to the carved woodwork and silk-covered furnishings.

SAFETY FIRST

In addition to opulent furnishings, the *Olympic* boasted state-of-the-art safety features. At the time, the *Olympic* was one of the safest ships to set sail. One magazine even called the White Star's new ships "practically unsinkable." But accidents and collisions are as old as the sea itself. And as the world soon learned, there is no such thing as an unsinkable ship. . . .

MAIDEN VOYAGE

The *Olympic*'s first trip went beautifully. White Star was happy with their new liner and the chairman even called her a "marvel."

The fancy ship interiors attracted rich customers. Once again, White Star controlled the largest share of the market. White Star's new fleet seemed to be doing well, but its luck was about to change.

BEGINNING OF BAD LUCK

On the *Olympic*'s fifth voyage, in a narrow channel near Southampton, England, the ship was passed by a Royal Navy cruiser, the H.M.S. *Hawke*. After pulling alongside the *Olympic*, the skipper of the *Hawke* discovered his controls were useless! His smaller boat was being drawn uncontrollably toward the enormous ship.

Unable to avoid the collision, the *Hawke* ripped through the *Olympic*'s side, slicing open a group of second-class cabins. Miraculously, nobody was killed.

Both ships limped back to port. Though the *Olympic* was blamed for the incident, the disaster was quickly forgotten . . . until a year later, when something eerily similar happened to the *Olympic*'s more famous sister ship.

TITANIC TWIN SISTER

On April 10, 1912, the *Titanic* was launched. She shared many similarities with the *Olympic*. Even some of the *Titanic*'s crew was the same — including Violet Jessop!

Violet, now a veteran steward, had been asked

to make the move from the *Olympic* to the *Titanic* and had eagerly agreed. She wanted to see how much more lavish than the *Olympic* the *Titanic* was. Violet was not disappointed. In addition to the many fancy finishing touches, the *Titanic* had small private decks, lace bedspreads, and exquisite woodcarvings from Ireland and Holland.

BAD OMEN

Unlike the *Olympic*, the *Titanic*'s launch did not draw too much publicity. And her maiden voyage in April 1912 almost ended before it began.

The same captain and pilot who had been sailing the *Olympic* when the *Hawke* crashed into her were sailing on the *Titanic* as she made her way out of the crowded Southampton channel. The *Titanic* was moving too fast and the *New York*, a boat that was tied nearby, was sucked toward the *Titanic*. The *New York* broke free of her moorings (all six lines snapped) and came within four feet of the *Titanic*'s stern before a tugboat caught and pulled her clear.

Though the collision was averted, there were whispers on board that the near miss was a bad omen. . . .

ICEBERG RIGHT AHEAD!

On the night of April 14, 1912, the *Titanic* met

her doom. A series of unfortunate mistakes — including warnings that went unheeded — led to her famous, fatal collision with an iceberg. The enormous ship sank in less than three hours. Only seven hundred people survived, while more than twice that many died in the icy waters of the Atlantic.

CURSED QUIZ

There were no boats close enough to come to the *Titanic*'s assistance when she began to sink.

True or false?

Answer: False. One ship was just ten miles away but did not hear the Titanic's distress calls. The telegraph operator on the other ship had gone to bed.

SURVIVOR

Among the survivors of the *Titanic* was Violet Jessop. As the ship was going down, she stood on deck, watching a young officer try to coax non-English-speaking immigrants to get into lifeboats. The poor officer could not make himself understood, so he asked some of his crewmates to illustrate his point. Violet climbed into a lifeboat to set a good example — and she saved her own life in the process!

THE THIRD SISTER

After the *Titanic* tragedy, White Star rushed to improve the safety features of the *Olympic*. They added more lifeboats, extended the watertight bulkheads, and made other changes as well. The *Olympic*'s changes were also added to her partially built sister ship, White Star's third and final Olympic-class liner.

SUNKEN TREASURE

When the *Titanic* went down, the ship took 3,364 sacks of mail, five grand pianos, and fifty cases of toothpaste with her.

After rigorous testing, the third sister ship was deemed seaworthy — with one final change: her name. After the *Titanic* went down, White Star decided that the planned name, *Gigantic*, might bring bad luck (since its meaning was so similar). So White Star called their last ship *Britannic* instead.

WARTIME

In August 1914, the *Britannic* was nearly set to sail the Atlantic with rich passengers on board when World War I broke out in Europe. Everything changed. The ship's maiden voyage was canceled, and like many ocean liners, the *Britannic* was forced into military service.

People all over the world volunteered for military service, too. One of them was none other than Violet Jessop!

After surviving collisions on both the *Titanic* and the *Olympic*, Violet was assigned to — you guessed it — the *Britannic*! She may have thought the *Britannic* would be luckier than her sister ships. But Violet was wrong.

CURSED QUIZ

The *Olympic* was one of the first ships to receive the frantic distress calls of the sinking *Titanic*.
True or false?

Answer: True. The Olympic was just five hundred miles away — sadly, too far to assist her sinking sister.

TIME TO REDECORATE?

Since the *Britannic* was still in the shipyard when war broke out, she was quickly refitted as a hospital ship. Her beautiful furnishings and works of art were replaced by hospital beds and medical equipment. She was also repainted with a green stripe and three red crosses. These markings were supposed to keep the *Britannic* safe from attack by German submarines while she collected wounded soldiers from the Greek island Lemnos and brought them back to England.

According to the Geneva Convention, an agreement signed by both sides of the war, hospital ships were safe from attack. But the ships had to follow certain rules. They were only allowed to transport medical staff and wounded, unarmed soldiers. Unfortunately the *Britannic* bent the rules a little and took medical combat troops to and from the front lines!

DEADLY MISTAKE

On the *Britannic*'s second voyage, the ship was rocked by a huge explosion. The crew rushed to the lifeboats and boarded them immediately. But the captain did not know the lifeboats had been launched and turned the ship sharply to try and beach it. It was an awful mistake.

The ship's enormous propellers broke the surface of the water and began to suck the lifeboats toward them. The massive blades continued to turn and the passengers and crew members aboard the lifeboats had to make a terrible choice: jump into the churning seas and take their chances, or face the sharp spinning blades — and certain death.

With the deadly blades nearly upon her, Violet Jessop jumped out of the lifeboat. She was dragged under by the suction. Then, to make matters worse, she cracked her skull on one of the other lifeboats. Dazed and terrified, Violet began to sink toward a watery grave.

However, at the last moment, Violet brushed the arm of another passenger, who pulled her to the surface. She had survived again.

Miraculously, of the more than one thousand people on board the *Britannic*, only thirty people died.

CURSED QUIZ

The ship that fueled the White Star and Cunard rivalry, the *Lusitania*, was sunk by a German submarine off the coast of Ireland. True or false?

Answer: True. The unarmed ship was sunk in 1915.

RUMORS

In spite of the safety improvements, the *Britannic* sank in only fifty-five minutes — almost three times faster than the Titanic! Why did she go down so fast? And more importantly, what caused the explosion?

There were many rumors. Some said *Britannic* was the victim of an ambush by a German torpedo. Germany told newspapers the *Britannic* was transporting medical combat personnel. There were even rumors of troops and weapons onboard.

The official Naval Inquiry didn't clear up any questions. It was done quickly and was incomplete. But the wreck faded into history as larger war news made headlines.

GRAND OLD LADY

About the same time the *Britannic* was turned into a floating hospital, the *Olympic* was converted into a troop transport. Painted in camouflage, she had many successful voyages. She even rammed and sank a German submarine (a pretty small target for a big, slow ship)!

SUNKEN TREASURE

By the time the furnishings, fixtures, and woodwork of the *Olympic* were sold at auctions, they were so old-fashioned hardly anyone wanted them. Still, you can see some of the ship's fittings in the White Swan Hotel in England. It uses the *Olympic's* interiors as décor.

One year later, the *Olympic* ended her military career and returned to her regular passenger route. Though she was never as popular as she had been before the war, the *Olympic* sailed for fifteen more years. She was even nicknamed the "Grand Old Lady of the North Atlantic" and "Old Reliable." Had she escaped the curse of her sisters?

NO SHRINKING VIOLET

When the *Olympic* went back to being a passenger ship, she had a familiar face serving onboard: Violet Jessop, of course! Though the brave steward had nearly gone down with both of the *Olympic's* sisters (and had a fear of drowning), Violet's horrific experiences couldn't keep her away from a good job!

Despite all her near misses, Violet Jessop did not die at sea. She eventually retired and passed away in 1971 at the age of eighty-four.

THE FIRST AND LAST

On May 15, 1934, the first of the White Star "triplets" to be launched made her final voyage. Coming into New York Harbor in the fog, bad luck finally caught up with the *Olympic* and she accidentally ran down a smaller ship, cutting it in two and killing several of the crew. One year later, the *Olympic* was sold for scrap.

SAILING AWAY

Though the *Titanic* and her sister ships are lost to us now, they have sailed into a special place in history. The *Titanic* in particular is the subject of numerous books and more than one movie! All three ships remain some of the best-known luxury liners of all time — in no small part because of their doomed and deadly destinies!

2

THE TOWER OF LONDON: A SINISTER HISTORY

The Tower of London has one of the bloodiest histories of any castle in the world. Today it houses the magnificent crown jewels of the royal family. But for centuries it housed enemies of the crown — many of whom met horrific deaths within its walls.

TOURISTS ... AND TORTURE!

The Tower of London is one of England's most popular tourist attractions. Each year more than two and a half million people come to be dazzled by the glittering jewels of the royal family. But if you were to come on a foggy, misty night, wander through the cold stone halls, and peek into the darkened cells, you might get *chills* instead of thrills. Within these stone walls, some of them nine hundred years old, many people were once imprisoned, tortured, and beheaded!

NINE HUNDRED YEARS AGO

In 1066, Norman forces swarmed across the English Channel to invade England. It was a bloody battle, but the Saxon (English) defenders were no match for the powerful Normans. The Norman horde took control of the country and proclaimed their leader, William the Conqueror, king.

William was the first to begin building the Tower of London. He chose a hill along the river Thames as his site — partly because the spot held the remains of an ancient Roman castle. Two sides of a tower were already in place. William's tower, called the White Tower, was built upon these existing walls.

William the Conqueror had two reasons for building his tower: to protect himself from his enemies and to show the English people that he was king.

From the outside, the Tower was impressive. But inside it was quite rugged. The royal family lived on the top floor and heated their quarters with an open fire. The next floor down held the royal court. Below that were the men at arms and the royal family's personal staff.

THE FIRST PRISONER

Even before construction was complete, the Tower received its first prisoner: Rannulf Flambard, the Bishop of Durham. As tax collector, Flambard had become quite wealthy — a little *too* wealthy for King William's liking.

But the clever Flambard was not a prisoner for long. As a person of high standing, he was allowed to have personal servants and special food and drink brought to the Tower. He quickly took advantage of this situation to engineer his escape.

Flambard had his servants bring in barrels. Most of them were filled with wine, but one of them held ropes. After generously sharing his wine with the guards (and getting them drunk), Flambard simply threw a rope out one of the Tower windows, climbed to the ground, and ran away!

CONDEMNED QUIZ

The mortar — a building material — in the first tower was colored by the blood of beasts.
True or false?

Answer: False. The rich red color actually came from crushed Roman tiles used in the cement.

THE LION TOWER

After William's rule, the next monarchs continued expanding the Tower of London. King Henry III enlarged the tower substantially, creating what is now called the Inner Curtain Wall. And within this Curtain, Henry III built several new structures that housed his garrison, armory, jewel house, wardrobe, currency mint, and even a menagerie (a kind of zoo)!

In 1235 Emperor Fredrick II presented King Henry with three leopards. Not long after that, the king of Norway gave Henry a polar bear. By 1276, King Henry had opened the Lion Tower to house his growing collection of animals. When visitors came to visit the king,

TOWER TIDBIT

When the king of Norway gave the polar bear to King Henry, he also gave him a rope and a collar. These were allegedly used to lead the bear to the river Thames so it could go swimming!

they first had to pass through the Lion Tower . . . if they dared!

A CITY WITHIN A CITY

Henry's son Edward I completed the outer walls of the castle when he built the Outer Curtain. The Tower now included twenty smaller towers and covered twelve acres. Hundreds of people lived and worked in the Tower, making it a small city in and of itself.

By the 1400s, the Tower of London was a lavish structure and very secure. It did not house many prisoners and few people were tortured inside. But trouble was brewing in England. Wealthy families struggled for power — and the kingdom.

TOWER TIDBIT

The most feared torture device in the Tower was called the rack. Prisoners were tied to the rack with rope by their hands and feet. When the winches were turned, their joints were dislocated. Ouch!

A BLOODY RULE

King Henry III, his son Edward I, and their descendants were all part of the Lancaster family. By the mid-1400s, the rule of the Lancaster family began to falter. King Henry VI was struck by a strange and debilitating disease. He lost control of his body and mind.

With the king weakened, the rival York family attacked the kingdom and laid claim to the throne. Shortly after that, the new king, Edward IV, imprisoned King Henry in the Wakefield Tower. Called "Mad Henry," the feeble king was mysteriously found dead at the foot of his prayer altar ten years later.

But even with the rival king permanently out of his way, King Edward was still on a mission to protect himself. No one was safe from his quest to

CONDEMNED QUIZ

The battle between the Yorks and the Lancasters was known as the War of the Roses because the coat of arms of both families feature roses. True or false?

Answer: True. The Lancastrian's is red and the York's is white.

silence his political enemies — not even his own brother!

In 1478, Edward locked his brother, George, in the Tower and sentenced him to death for treason. George was known to be a heavy drinker, and his death was carried out in a very unusual way: He was drowned in a giant tub of wine!

During Edward IV's rule, the Tower housed prisoners from all over England. Many were beheaded on Tower Hill. Others were simply locked away — some with comfortable furnishings, and others without clothing or ample food. But all of the prisoners of the Tower had one thing in common: boredom. With too much time on their hands, many used whatever instruments they could find to carve inscriptions on the Tower's stone walls. The carvings are still there today!

A MOST EVIL UNCLE

When King Edward IV died in 1483, his thirteen-year-old son, Edward, was named king. Edward's uncle, the Duke of Gloucester, was assigned to be his protector. Instead, the duke unlawfully took the throne, naming himself King Richard III.

Young Edward and his brother were imprisoned in a secure section of the Tower . . . until one day they disappeared altogether.

Rumors went around that the boys had been murdered. It was believed that King Richard ordered two men to suffocate the boys in their sleep and dispose of the bodies under a pile of rubble at the foot of the stairs. And that is exactly where, in 1674, a chest containing human bones was found!

TOWER TIDBIT

Perhaps the worst part of being a prisoner in the Tower was your uncertain fate. You never knew if you would be freed or executed — it all depended on the king's mood!

Just two years after having his nephews murdered, King Richard was killed in battle. His violent rule came to an abrupt end. But his successor, Henry Tudor, ushered in the bloodiest dynasty in the Tower's history!

KING HENRY THE HORRIBLE

King Henry VIII assumed the throne in 1509. By now the king of England did not live in the Tower, as it had fallen into disrepair. But the

Tower was still a prison, and since Henry VIII did not have a son to succeed him, he filled it with anyone whom he thought might attempt to lay claim to the throne.

Among Henry's prisoners was his own wife, Anne Boleyn. At the time of her execution, Anne and Henry VIII had been married for three years and had one child, a daughter. Furious that she had not given him an heir (only sons could inherit the throne at the time), Henry had Anne taken to the Tower and had her beheaded!

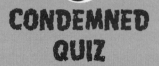

CONDEMNED QUIZ

According to legend, when Anne Boleyn's severed head was raised, her eyes and lips actually moved.
True or false?

Answer: True!

Six years later, King Henry VIII's fifth wife, Catherine Howard, was also beheaded. But the final victim condemned by Henry VIII, the Duke of Norfolk, suddenly got lucky. The night before the duke was to be executed, King Henry VIII died in his sleep!

KA-BOOM!

Though it was not common knowledge, the Tower housed most of London's gunpowder. In 1666, fire broke out in the streets of London.

Wind-whipped, the roaring blaze quickly spread toward the Tower of London . . . and its secret, deadly contents. A single spark in the wrong place could mean an explosion — and the destruction of a centuries-old structure.

The flames crept closer. Frantic, the Tower officials agreed to a radical plan. Using the gunpowder, they blew up the surrounding buildings in an attempt to save the Tower itself.

It worked. The rubble from the demolished buildings created a firebreak. But although the Tower was saved, the four-day fire destroyed much of the rest of London.

ANOTHER ERA

The newly rebuilt London was a great, modern city. Though the Tower was still filled with prisoners, torture had fallen out of favor. It was a more genteel era, a time of elegance and grace. It was also an era of prison escapes. . . .

THE TWO "LADY" NITHSDALES

The most famous and unique escape from the Tower was that of Scotsman William Maxwell, Earl of Nithsdale. In 1716, Maxwell was involved in a plot to dethrone King George I. Along with several others, he was brought to the Tower and condemned to death!

When she heard of her husband's arrest, Lady Nithsdale traveled to London to plead for mercy from King George. When the king ignored her pleas, Lady Nithsdale came up with another sort of plan.

With the help of two of her maids, Lady Nithsdale orchestrated her husband's escape. Wearing extra coats so as to appear larger than they were, the three women moved in and out of the earl's room, sobbing bitterly into their handkerchiefs. They came and went, weeping, for days, until the guards barely noticed them anymore. Then Lady Nithsdale disguised her husband with heavy makeup and a wig she had brought in under her coat. Dressed like a woman, Lord Nithsdale walked right past the jailers, sobbing bitterly. The guards, of course, never noticed!

To complete the ruse, Lady Nithsdale stayed behind in the cell, carrying on a pretend conversation with her husband. Then, upon leaving, she locked the door from the inside and instructed the servants not to disturb her husband during his prayer. By the time the escape was discovered, the Nithsdales had fled safely to Rome!

WAR AND PEACE

In 1837, Queen Victoria ascended to the throne. By this time in British history, a woman who was the rightful heir to the throne (the daughter of the previous king) was allowed to become queen. Queen Victoria's crowning marked the beginning of the Victorian era.

After the start of the Victorian era, the Tower became a tourist attraction, settling into a quieter, more dignified life. Only World Wars I and II forced the castle back to its official duty as a state prison.

In World War I, the Tower housed eleven German spies who were later killed by firing squad. During World War II, the lower levels of the Tower served as an air raid shelter, a protected place where people hid when bombs or other explosives were dropped from military aircraft. The Tower also served as a victory garden, a place where everyday people grew vegetables to feed themselves during wartime.

TOWER TIDBIT

Pet ravens have been kept on the Tower grounds for more than a hundred years. One was named Ronnie Raven, after U.S. President Ronald Reagan!

Extensive bombing by Nazi planes destroyed much of the Tower of London during World War II. But these bombings also had a positive result: They unearthed original Tower walls built as early as the thirteenth century! Archaeologists today see the Tower as a layer cake, with unknown mysteries still hidden in its walls and under its floors.

Indeed, the Tower of London has a fascinating — if sometimes gruesome! — history. No longer a place of torture, its walls and floors remain rich with the glory of England's past and present. Today, you can easily visit the Tower if you are in London. And although it may seem creepy, you'll have nothing to fear—you won't get stuck there as a prisoner now!

CRYPTS, COFFINS, AND CORPSES:
REMAINS OF THE DEAD

What should the living do with the dead? It's a question that has concerned people across the ages. When a person dies, their body remains on earth. Throughout history, cultures have handled the bodies of the deceased in different ways. From ancient mummification to sending remains into outer space, the way we say good-bye to our dead has been both varied and bizarre. . . .

HANDLING THE DEAD

One thing in life has always been certain: death. Life does not go on forever. And when a person dies, the living must decide what to do with the remains. In ancient Egypt, mummification was common. In Europe, people have been buried in the ground for centuries. And cremation, or burning, has also found its place in many death rituals. But how and where did these and other traditions begin?

WHAT'S THAT SMELL?

For prehistoric man, disposing of a dead body quickly was a priority. A few days after a person died, the body would start to smell. This was not only unpleasant, it could also bring wild animals and other predators to the space of the living. So early man usually did one of four things: buried the body in the ground, covered it with rocks, moved to a nearby cave, or left the area entirely.

MUMMIFY ME

The ancient Egyptians (who lived approximately between the years 3000 B.C. and 300 B.C.) developed a much more elaborate method of dealing with the dead: mummification. High priests of the time began to think of dead bodies as having souls that could live on, and loved ones wanted to protect those souls as best they could.

There are different kinds of mummification, and Egyptian mummification was one of the most complicated. First the vital organs were removed from the body. Then the corpse was bathed in salt, wrapped in oil-soaked linens, and left to rest for seventy days. What remained was a tough, tanned layer of skin covering bones and muscle.

Once a mummy was prepared, it was placed in an elaborate, often colorful case called a sarcophagus — in a sense, the first kind of coffin. The sarcophagi were placed in tombs in great pyramids along with the deceased's most treasured earthly possessions. Pharaohs, or kings, were often buried with large amounts of gold and jewels!

QUICK CREMATION

Bodies have been burned since the Stone Age. In India, funeral pyres have lit up the skies for centuries. But the ancient Greeks were the first to make a ritual out of the burning of corpses, which is known as cremation. The Greeks believed that a soul could only move

DEADLY DETAIL

During the Middle Ages, Tibetans had an unusual way of dealing with their dead. They put the bodies in a temple and let dogs devour them! Although this may sound gruesome to us, the Tibetans saw it as a holy rite of passage.

on to the next life if it were completely free of the body — if the body itself was destroyed.

Later, during the Middle Ages (the time period from A.D. 500 to 1500), cremation became popular for another reason. Life at the time was difficult and often short. Plagues and wars left thousands of people dead. Burning the corpses seemed like the easiest way to dispose of the many bodies. But there was an environmental problem. In order to cremate a body you needed an exceptionally hot fire, and the only way to make one was to burn a lot of wood. With so many bodies to dispose of, the forests were being depleted. Little lumber was left for building and heating homes!

CORPSE QUIZ

Cremation is encouraged in India because many people throw their dead into the Ganges River, causing the waterway to be filled with corpses. True or false?

Answer: True. Throwing a body into the river is considered the holiest burial, but the tradition is creating environmental problems.

Over time, modern methods of cremation have developed. Cremation is now fast, clean, and odorless. Flames do not touch the body. It is heat alone that consumes the corpse — heat at temperatures between 1,600 and 1,800 degrees Fahrenheit! The ashes are generally placed in an urn, and may rest there or be sprinkled in a special place by the loved ones of the deceased.

Today, about twenty-five percent of the bodies in the United States are cremated. Most of the rest are handled in another age-old manner . . . burial.

SIX FEET UNDER

More than two thousand years ago, the most common method of handling a dead body was pioneered in a far corner of the Roman Empire. The method was burial — putting a dead body deep into the ground. At first, bodies were buried in caves. But by the Middle Ages, a different burial site was popular: churches. Families wanted their loved ones to be close to God, even in death. So corpses were prepared, brought to the local church, and laid to rest under stone slabs in the floor. This seemed to work

DEADLY DETAIL

The Vikings practiced a horrifying ritual. Not only did they burn their dead, they also sacrificed living friends and relatives by throwing them into the funeral fire!

well for a time . . . until the bodies began to decompose and smell bad.

To rid the churches of the dead and still keep the bodies close to God, Europeans developed the cemetery — a special area just for the bodies that was right outside the church. This was an improvement, but with so many decomposing bodies still in one area, churchyards were not pleasant places to visit!

It was not until the 1800s that larger cemeteries were created. No longer associated with the church, these cemeteries were almost like parks, with wide lawns, trees, and flowers. Some featured huge monuments honoring the dead. But along with these beautiful cemeteries came a sinister fear. People became terrified of being buried alive!

GET ME OUT OF HERE!

Writers of the 1800s spun tales of people waking up six feet underground in hard wooden boxes, unable to get out! This was not really a new fear, but one that had existed for centuries. Long ago, people did not have modern tools to diagnose death. A person in a coma could be mistaken for dead. So the body in question was placed in a cave and visited for three days. If it began to rot, it was dead, and the cave was sealed until the next burial. Watching a body in a cave was an easy way to make sure someone was dead. Without a waiting period, it was more likely that a person would be accidentally buried alive.

CORPSE QUIZ

In ancient Greece, people would dig up loved ones on the anniversary of their death and throw parties with the corpse as the guest of honor! True or false?

Answer: False. Though the practice is true, it actually took place in Mexico and Madagascar during the first millennium.

In the nineteenth century, rumors of people waking up underground began to spread. So coffin makers of the time devised clever devices to soothe a nervous public. Some coffins had escape hatches. Others featured windows that would fog up if the person inside was still breathing. Still others were rigged with a string a person could pull if they woke up underground. The string was attached to a bell aboveground. Pulling the string would cause the bell to ring and be a sure sign that the buried person was alive!

A NEW METHOD

Until the mid-1800s, most bodies were buried right away — without being treated — and rotted slowly in the ground. But the American Civil War brought about changes in how a newly dead body was handled. Tens of thousands of young men lost their lives in battle, and families wanted their boys sent home and laid to rest. But the families also wanted to see their loved ones intact, to say good-bye one last time.

But how do you preserve a body for transport back to a grieving family? President Lincoln urged battlefield surgeons to make use of a new method called embalming — replacing human blood with chemicals.

Dr. Thomas Holmes was the first doctor to perfect embalming on the battlefront. But before he would begin the procedure on a body, he buried the soldier and sent a letter to the family to see if

DEADLY DETAIL

It took a full construction crew and two cement trucks to bury oil heiress Sandra Ilene West. That's because she was buried sitting behind the wheel of her 1964 Ferrari!

they wanted, and could pay for, the embalming. If they did, he dug up the corpse and got to work.

While draining the blood from the body, Dr. Holmes used a hand pump to pump a new, arsenic-rich fluid into the veins and arteries. Though a deadly poison, arsenic is an amazing preservative of human flesh. (Today, arsenic has been replaced with formaldehyde, which poses less danger to the embalmer.) The bodies of Civil War soldiers could now be sent home to their families.

PRESIDENTIAL PRESERVATION

Interestingly, when President Lincoln was assassinated in 1865, he himself was embalmed. It was twenty-one days after his death that he arrived home in Springfield, Illinois, because he went on a kind of funeral parade.

Lincoln's embalmed corpse traveled more than 1,700 miles through major cities such as New York and Chicago. In each city his body was displayed to the public, who grieved at the loss of their leader. This procession was, in fact, one of the first modern funerals. From this point on in history, people began to have public services and ceremonies to mourn their dead.

MODERN AND MYSTERIOUS

In the last several decades, new and strange methods of dealing with the dead have emerged. A scientist named Robert C. W. Ettinger began to freeze bodies in the hopes of bringing them back to life in the future. Most scientists agree that this process, called reanimation, is a science-fiction idea that will never become a reality. Still, some people choose this method of preservation — just in case.

DEADLY DETAIL

President George Washington's body was also preserved, but in a different way. It was left to freeze in an unheated parlor until his family could travel to his burial!

Today, a Houston-based company called Celestis launches the cremated remains of people into space, where they will orbit for thirty to forty years! And as for those who continue to be buried, some are more beautifully preserved than ever — especially in the United States. Schools such as the San Francisco College of Mortuary Science teach involved corpse preparation techniques. First the body is preserved with formaldehyde. Then it is bathed, the hair is shampooed, and the fingernails are cleaned and trimmed. Cosmetics are applied to make the person look lifelike. All of this preparation allows family members to see the deceased one last time, looking attractive and restful.

A WAY TO SAY GOOD-BYE

Over time, people have said good-bye to loved ones in many different ways. From funeral pyres to church graveyards, from frozen bodies to capsules sent into outer space, our rituals are as varied as our cultures and religious backgrounds. But for all of us, one thing is the same. Death rituals have become more than ways to simply dispose of bodies. The special rites and customs allow us to say good-bye to those we care about, and to remember those who have gone before us.

4

CLIFF MUMMIES OF PERU:
SEARCHING FOR ANCIENT SECRETS

High in the mountains of northeastern Peru, an ancient people buried their mummified dead in the sheer cliffs of this unwelcoming terrain. The practices of these ancient people are shrouded in mystery, but modern archaeologists have embarked on a spooky and difficult journey to unearth clues—and long-buried mummies! Join us as we seek out the secrets of the Chachapoya.

PEOPLE OF THE CLOUDS

The Chachapoya (chah-chah-PO-ya) are a mysterious, ancient people. Though many would consider the region they settled—called the cordillera—uninhabitable, the Chachapoya made it their home. Honing shingles by hand, they built massive fortresses and small cities. They created flat gardening spaces out of steep mountain slopes. And high in the nearby vertical cliffs, they buried their mummified dead!

Since they lived at ten and eleven thousand feet, the Chachapoya were often surrounded by cloudy mists that shrouded the rocky peaks. They were in many ways a "people of the clouds," which is what some historians believe "Chachapoya" means.

MUMMY PROTECTORS

The Chachapoya believed that the elders of the community possessed great wisdom. So when the elders died, the community mummified their bodies, wrapping them in their handmade, finely woven textiles. Then they placed the bodies in dry caves high in the mountain cliffs. Items such as bowls, baskets, and drinking gourds were left in the caves with the mummies. Wealthy or important mummies were adorned with jewelry, possibly even gold.

From their mountain resting places, the mummies looked down on the Chachapoya people, protecting them. The mummies were consulted about tribal issues. Some people even paid taxes to mummies. It was almost as if the Chachapoya believed their mummified ancestors were still alive!

THE FIGHT FOR POWER

Archaeologists believe that the Chachapoya were a warring people who fought among themselves. They surrounded their buildings with defensive boundaries, and an ancient pictograph outside one of the cliff tombs shows somebody holding the head of a decapitated victim!

Nobody knows why the Chachapoya fought one another. Perhaps they battled over land. Other evidence suggests that their shamans fought one another for power. Many clever witch doctors were practicing during the Chachapoya's time, and some evidence indicates that they worked hard to cast spells and hexes on one another!

INCA INVASION

In addition to the intertribal battles, other, outside people wanted to steal the Chachapoya's land.

Here is a painting of the famously doomed ship the *Titanic*.
Just five days after its launch from Southampton, England,
on April 10, 1912, the grand ocean liner would meet its
watery doom....

The *Titanic*'s sister ships—the *Olympic* and the *Britannic*—
looked almost identical to the *Titanic,* and all three ships
eventually encountered disaster on the high seas.

THE HISTORY CHANNEL®

The remarkable Violet Jessop, shown here on board the ship *Orinoco*, worked as a stewardess on the *Olympic*, the *Titanic*, and the *Britannic*—and she miraculously survived life-threatening accidents on all three ships!

Welcome to the Tower of London! Below is a photo of some of the ancient buildings that make up the legendary Tower. This popular tourist attraction of today was once a notorious and frightening prison. The photo above shows some markings that desperate prisoners carved into walls of the Tower long ago....

Jonathan Blair/Corbis

Buddy Mays/Corbis

THE HISTORY CHANNEL.

King Henry VIII is one of the most infamous royal figures associated with the Tower of London. He imprisoned several people in the Tower and had two of his wives beheaded there!

THE HISTORY CHANNEL.

This is an example of an ancient Egyptian sarcophagus—the first-ever kind of coffin. Some ancient Egyptians put their mummified dead into colorful sarcophagi and then placed those sarcophagi inside the great pyramids.

While ancient Egyptians made use of sarcophagi, most modern-day peoples place their dead in coffins—such as the one shown here in the back of a hearse. Coffins are taken to cemeteries, then buried deep in the ground.

Stone/Getty

This is a photo of a Chachapoyan mummy, dating from between A.D. 500 and 1000, after it has been unwrapped from its wooden burial coffin in a museum in Peru. Keith Muscutt and his brave team were lucky to discover mummies of this sort during their difficult journey through the cliffs of Peru.

Here is a cemetery during nightfall. In the eighteenth and nineteenth century in England and America, body snatchers (usually medical students in need of corpses) would use the darkness of night to sneak into graveyards . . . and dig up some of the dead!

Mark Keller/SuperStock

Though the land was extremely rugged, it was also very valuable, because the Chachapoya controlled the trade routes between the coastal deserts of the Pacific and the Amazon Basin to the east. And the Incas, people living in a rising empire south of the Chachapoya, wanted control over those trade routes. In the mid-1400s, the Incas attacked the Chachapoya.

The Chachapoya fought back. But because the Chachapoya were not a united force, one town after another was overtaken by the Incas. The defeated Chachapoya were moved to other parts of the Incan empire. But they were not happy, and they tried to make life for the Incas as miserable as possible.

A MYSTERIOUS KILLER

About fifty years after the Chachapoya were defeated, the Inca ruler, Huayna Capac, suddenly died.

TOMB TRIVIA

Not all the Chachapoya burial practices were the same. Some deceased were simply mummified and placed in caves. Others were put into decorative stone coffins. Still others were housed in multistoried "houses" with windows and doors!

Many Incas thought that a Chachapoyan shaman had come across the oceans with European explorers. The Incas and the Chachapoya were strong people. But they did not have any immunity to these new diseases. And when the Spaniards landed in South America in the 1500s, they brought with them even *more* illnesses.

had poisoned him. But historians today believe that the Incan and his family were killed by something even more deadly: a disease that

CLIFF QUIZ

According to legend, both the Incas and the Chachapoya hid their gold from the Spaniards by throwing it into sacred lakes. True or false?

Answer: True. Some archaeologists believe it is still there!

SPANISH INVASION

The Spaniards came to the Americas in search of gold, for it was rumored that the land was filled with riches. In 1532, Spanish captain Francisco Pizarro landed in Peru. Wielding their guns and swords and riding horses, Pizarro and his small Spanish army defeated the Incas within hours . . . with the help of the Chachapoya! Still furious at the Incas for taking their land, the Chachapoya saw the Spaniards as their rescuers.

Little did the Chachapoya know that within a few years the Spaniards would imprison *them* in their mines and fields *and* loot their sacred burial grounds for gold and other precious metals. The diseases the Spaniards brought with them from Europe — smallpox and influenza — would kill off nearly three quarters of the Chachapoyan population.

FORGOTTEN VILLAGES

The few Chachapoya who survived the epidemics of European diseases lived out their days in Spanish settlements. Located in remote areas, these settlements remained basically the same for nearly five hundred years and came to be known as the "forgotten villages." One of them, called Uchucmarca (oochook-MAR-ka), is eighteen hours by car from the nearest city! And the road to Uchucmarca was built only a few years ago.

CLIFF QUIZ

Chachapoyan tomb builders wove ropes from *ten-foot* strands of wild mountain grass. True or false?

Answer: False. The mountain grass only grew to three feet, not ten — but the tomb builders did use it to make ropes.

Since then, present-day campesinos — peasant farmers and ranchers — have resettled this remote area. They soon discovered the ancient Chachapoyan burial sights and many of them robbed the tombs for the mummies' valuables. Today, nearly all of the cliff tombs have been looted for treasure, so hardly any remain untouched.

MUSCUTT'S MISSION

With a team of experienced climbers, some campesino scouts, and a few mules, author/photographer Keith Muscutt decided to set off on a new expedition in search of undisturbed mummies. Prior to this expedition, Muscutt had found hundreds of cliff tombs. But he had not yet found one that *hadn't* been looted!

TOMB TRIVIA

Only one thing keeps looters from the cliff tombs: Mummy Disease! The air in the tombs, called antimonia, is said to cause dizziness, nausea, bleeding, and even death!

A TRICKY TREK

Muscutt, climber Herb Laeger, and photographer Richard Leversee had their work cut out for them. Even with professional climbing gear, the cliff sites were hard to reach. Just to get to the cliffs they had to travel ten hours by mule, climb over a 12,500-foot mountain pass, and traverse wet tundra that nearly stopped the mules in their tracks.

CLIFF QUIZ

Once a year, during Christmas, entire Peruvian villages loot cave sites. The campesinos believe that during this time, looters are safe from evil spirits that might be lurking in the caves. True or false?

Answer: False. They do it during Easter week.

The group was headed for a lake, Laguna Huayabamba (Lah-GU-na WHY-ah-bahm-ba), situated at ten thousand feet. Surrounding the lake were cliff faces more than six hundred feet high! And nearby was the ancient Chachapoyan fortress Vira Vira.

Muscutt chose to search for mummies in this area for several reasons. First, it was located in a place that was difficult to travel to, which would make it difficult for looters to get to. Second, the Spaniards had never established villages here. And because Vira Vira was so big, Muscutt suspected that many dead would have been buried in the nearby cliffs — so the chances of finding un-looted tombs were better.

A SHAKY START

From base camp, Muscutt and his fellow climbers hiked up to Vira Vira and the large circular main building. From there they used telescopes to search the lakeside cliffs for signs of tombs.

Right away Muscutt spotted an arched red pictograph, a sign that cliff sites could be nearby. And just a few feet away, high in the cliff, were signs of construction.

Excited about the possibility of a big discovery, the crew wasted no time getting down to the lake. Then Laeger and Leversee began the perilous climb to the tomb, using a cordless drill to anchor bolts to the cliff face. Below, Muscutt listened to the activity via radio. As Laeger closed in on the tomb, anticipation grew. Would there be undisturbed mummies inside?

TOMB TRIVIA

At breakfast on the first day of the exploration, Muscutt was served a ram's head — a delicacy in Peru — which he happily ate!

Finally Laeger could see into the tomb. But he found absolutely nothing. The cave was empty.

Fortunately, there was another tomb farther up the cliff face. This time Leversee led the climb. Instead of placing additional bolts into the cliff wall, he free-climbed. He was wearing a harness and was attached to a rope, but if he fell, it would be a long way down before the anchors Laeger had placed would stop him in midair!

Leversee moved carefully along the rock face, looking for hand- and footholds. He scrambled up to a ledge in front of the cliff tomb. Finally he got a look inside. But, as before, there was nothing to be found.

In spite of the disappointment, the group kept searching. Below them was a third cave. Laeger made his way toward it, kicking rocks loose as he climbed. Inside, he found several human bones! But nothing was intact. The space had definitely been a tomb, but it had been looted.

The next day brought even more disappoint-ment. So on the third day, the men moved the search to the opposite side of the lake. The campesino scouts had spotted a red cliff there.

Before the climbers made their way up to the tomb, one of the scouts made an offering to the spirits. Then Leversee scaled the cliff to look inside. Keith and the scouts climbed up to see what was there, too. But yet again . . . the tomb was empty.

A SURPRISING DISCOVERY

After three days of fruitless searching, the team was feeling frustrated. Muscutt wondered if they were searching for nothing.

At Laeger's suggestion, the team headed to a large cave at the head of the lake. But on their way there, the team noticed a few things. The ground was covered with ash from a large fire, and skulls and bones were strewn about.

Making their way to a low, manmade wall in the cliff, the team at last found a communal

TOMB TRIVIA

Were the bodies in the communal grave that Laeger found commoners who died naturally but did not get their own gravesites? Were they victims of a disease epidemic? With careful study of the area, archaeologists hope to find out!

grave! The remains of hundreds of bodies were piled together. The site had been looted, but with pieces of cloth visible and the bones of so many in one place, it was still a valuable discovery.

ANOTHER EXCITING FIND

Leaving the mass grave, Laeger and Leversee climbed up and into the large cave. They found delicate iciclelike formations, but no signs of human activity. Then, as they began their descent, something caught their attention. It was a jumble of rocks that looked like the entrance to a tomb and wasn't visible from the ground because of the shrubs and bushes.

Because it was late in the day, the explorers decided to wait until morning to explore the site. Would the wait be worth it?

The next morning the threesome — without the campesino scouts — made their way to the new site. Though it was only twenty feet off the ground, it was a tricky climb.

Inside the tomb they found ten mummies wrapped in cotton textiles, as well as several other skulls and bones. The site even held undisturbed baskets and ceramic dishes. Finally Laeger had made his discovery — an intact tomb!

Laeger and his teammates were thrilled with their discovery. But in order to keep the tomb safe, they had to keep it a secret. They did not tell the scouts about their discovery. They hid their trail as best they could. Then Muscutt petitioned the National Institute of Culture to excavate the tomb and move the mummies to a place where they could be studied. Fortunately, the tomb was not looted while Laeger waited for permission from the institute. The mummies were safely moved.

WHAT'S NEXT?

Keith Muscutt's discovery near Laguna Huayabamba was major — a remarkable piece of Chachapoyan heritage was discovered. But a lot of work still lies ahead. From those ten bodies wrapped in textiles archaeologists need to coax answers to big questions: Who were they? How did they die? How were they mummified?

There is still much to learn about the Chachapoya civilization. But finding ancient, untouched Chachapoyan mummies is an amazing step toward learning more about this resourceful, independent people and their fascinating way of life.

BODY SNATCHERS: DIGGING UP THE TRUTH

Imagine a cemetery on a moonless night. A shadowy figure digs in the freshly turned earth. His prize? A dead body!

Grave robbers might sound like something from a made-up ghost story, but they're not! In eighteenth- and nineteenth-century England and America, body snatchers were very real. Were these ghoulish criminals simply greedy and heartless, or did they provide a valuable service toward the development of modern medicine? Read on to discover the truth behind the body snatchers.

OLD-TIME MEDICINE

Compared to our very advanced modern medical knowledge, medicine in the eighteenth century seems pretty primitive. In eighteenth-century England, if you needed surgery or wanted a shave, you would see the same person! Medicine was practiced by "barber-surgeons." These doctors would "bleed" their patients, removing what they thought was unhealthy blood — often leaving the patients weak and sicker. And the doctors would perform surgery without anesthesia. Their patients could feel everything!

As one might imagine, aspiring barber-surgeons received little if any training. This was largely due to the lack of human bodies available for study. The Company of Barbers and Surgeons was only allowed four bodies a year for medical classes, so their students graduated and went into practice without ever dissecting a human body firsthand.

BODIES WANTED!

A few medical pioneers realized that the lack of bodies available to medical students was a real problem. To understand how a body worked, the students needed to look inside. Back then, before X rays or other advanced technology, one of the few ways people had of learning about the body was to dissect it.

In 1749, John and William Hunter opened a

new medical school using the "Parisian" curriculum. Under their system, every student was required to dissect a body before they could graduate. The system worked well in France, where any unclaimed body in a hospital or poorhouse could be used for dissection. But in England, where only four bodies a year were available, there was a severe shortage of bodies to study.

Where could English medical teachers and students go to get cadavers?

COFFIN QUIZ

Getting a glimpse inside a body used to be so rare that dissections were done in huge theaters where students and the public could watch. The dissections were advertised on posters and people would wait in line for hours to see them!
True or false?

Answer: True.

NO DISSECTION, PLEASE

In 1752, the College of Surgeons petitioned the government for more bodies. Parliament, England's governing electorate, responded with the Act to Prevent the Horrid Crime of Murder. The act stated that all hanged murderers must either be displayed on the gibbet or handed over to medical schools for dissection. Before being hanged, the prisoners were given the choice — and hardly any of them chose dissection. They were afraid that they still might live — and wake up on the table!

BIRTH OF BODY SNATCHING

Parliament's act did not help to supply schools with many more bodies. Meanwhile, medical schools were attracting more students. The body shortage was more severe than ever. If medical school teachers couldn't provide corpses, their schools would close!

Finally, medical school instructors were forced to take matters into their own hands. Instructors soon found themselves in local graveyards, digging up cadavers. These first grave robbers became known as "gentleman body snatchers." And strangely enough, what they were doing wasn't illegal! Nobody owned a body, so as long as the snatcher left every shred of clothing, shrouds, and sheets in the grave, he was in the clear. But if the

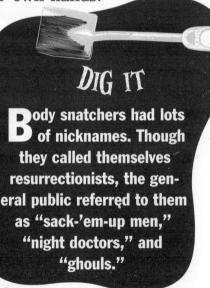

DIG IT

Body snatchers had lots of nicknames. Though they called themselves resurrectionists, the general public referred to them as "sack-'em-up men," "night doctors," and "ghouls."

snatcher accidentally left with so much as a sock, the theft was considered a serious offense!

WHO LIES HERE?

Stealing bodies wasn't an easy job. It was backbreaking work and had to be done at night without causing a stir. Body snatchers had to act fast. Since only fresh corpses were good for dissection, graves had to be robbed within ten days of burial.

Using wooden spades because they were quieter than metal, the robbers would dig a hole just over the head of the casket. Then they would pry off the top half of the coffin lid and pull the body out using a rope. Although taking a body wasn't illegal, it was certainly frowned upon. If graves in a cemetery were noticeably disturbed, guards would be posted to stop future pilfering. And the dead person's angry relatives sometimes beat up body snatchers who were caught!

Grave robbers' most popular targets were potter's fields, where the poor and orphaned were buried. The graves there were shallower and not as well-kept, making them both easier to dig and less likely to be noticed after they were robbed.

COMING TO AMERICA

In 1765, William Shippen Jr., a graduate of the Hunter's School in England, became an anatomy instructor for the first medical college in America (at the University of Pennsylvania). He, too, began practicing body snatching as a way to study cadavers. But the taboos against dissection were as strong in America as they had been in England. When word got out that Shippen was stealing bodies for dissection, a mob attacked his house!

DIG IT

The shortage of bodies in New York's medical schools wasn't handled in the courts until 1854, when students were allowed to take unclaimed bodies from the city morgue.

As more medical schools opened and more cadavers were needed, the public's dislike of medical schools and physicians grew. At New York Hospital, students foolishly teased passing children by dangling amputated body parts out the classroom windows. One little boy, whose mother had recently died, ran to tell his father. When his father returned to see what was going on, he had a mob with him. The angry crowd stormed the school, destroying equipment and threatening teachers and students.

Though the riot did not end until the militia was called and several protesters had been killed, it did result in a new anatomy law. The new law authorized dissections on the unclaimed bodies of executed criminals only. Though it was a first step, it still did not provide enough bodies for medical students.

NEW BREED OF BODY SNATCHERS

In 1788, back in England, doctors encountered a new problem. According to a new ruling, it was a legally punishable offense to steal a body. Unwilling to face jail time, most anatomy instructors stopped digging for cadavers.

But many criminals in England soon realized that there was money to be made in the business of body snatching. Digging up a body and selling it to a surgeon was a lot less risky than breaking into houses or holding up rich people. It did not take long for body snatching to catch on in the criminal world. . . .

CORPSE KING

One crook, Ben Crouch, soon became the top body snatcher in England. A buyer and seller of stolen goods and an illegal fight promoter, Crouch and his band of tough ex-boxers quickly cornered the market on medical cadavers.

Known as the "corpse king," Crouch and his gang squashed the competition by beating them up or giving the police secret information about them. If Crouch discovered a gang had a hold on one of the cemeteries, he and his boys would go in and trash it — throwing bones and remains all over!

After eliminating the competition, Crouch kept prices up by limiting the number of bodies available. He was a smart businessman and forced medical schools to sign exclusive contracts with him or risk having no bodies for a year.

DIG IT

If the supply of corpses in England ran low, the Crouch gang would import bodies from Ireland packed in whiskey-filled kegs marked PICKLES and HAMS.

BODY BATTLES

In a short time, medical instructors became totally dependent on the criminal body snatchers they employed. Even though their activities were illegal, body snatchers like Ben Crouch were a sure way to get cadavers. But instructors grew increasingly unhappy about the prices they were forced to pay. Medical instructors formed the Anatomists Club and tried to set the price of a body. The bitter back-and-forth battles that resulted between anatomists and body snatchers were called the "resurrectionist wars."

The wars raged until 1816, when Crouch demanded higher fees from doctors at Middlesex Hospital. When the doctors refused, Crouch's gang terrorized students in the dissecting room and destroyed the bodies in the mortuary. When the criminals were arrested, Crouch threatened to make public what was going on. The doctors quickly dropped the charges and paid Crouch and his partner huge sums of money.

REMEMBER TO LOCK THAT COFFIN!

All of the attention given to the resurrectionist wars brought body snatching into the public eye. Soon products designed to stop body snatching appeared on the market. Coffins with locks, metal cages that fit over graves, and iron straps that held bodies in coffins were advertised. But none of the expensive new inventions caught on.

GRIM AND GRIMMER

In 1827, in Scotland, an elderly renter died in his apartment. This occurrence would eventually lead to the end of body snatching.

The man's landlord, William Hare, decided that since the renter owed him rent, Hare would sell the body to get money! Hare and his friend William Burke took the body to a medical instructor named Dr. Knox. The men were thrilled to get ten gold coins for it. Normally it would take them months to earn so much money! This gave them an evil idea: Why *wait* for the tenants to die?

Soon Burke and Hare were showing up regularly at Dr. Knox's door with dead bodies. Dr. Knox was thrilled with his new source of cadavers. He wondered why the corpses were so fresh, but didn't want to probe too deeply into his good fortune.

Burke and Hare murdered and sold more than sixteen victims before they were caught in 1828.

COFFIN QUIZ

Body snatchers made money on the side selling teeth to dentists. True or false?

Answer: True. Dentists used the teeth to make dentures.

Burke was convicted and hanged before a crowd of 100,000. Hare got a more lenient sentence for testifying against his partner. Then, of course, Burke's own body was dissected!

ANATOMY ACT

Burke and Hare weren't the only people to think of killing to make money off bodies. Three years after the Burke trial, three men in London began to drug and then drown victims. They were called the Bethnal Green Gang, and the huge public outrage when they were caught finally forced Parliament to take action. Parliament passed the Anatomy Act, which stated that local authorities could hand over bodies from the workhouses to surgeons and that every body would be inspected to see where it came from. Body snatching in England "died" overnight.

DIG IT

After William Burke's exploits, people started to use the word "burking." Originally, the word meant "to suffocate" since Burke smothered most of his victims. Today "to burke" means to suppress something.

SNATCHING IN AMERICA

It took forty more years and even more outrage to bring anatomy reform to the United States. In 1878, John Scott Harrison, the father of President Benjamin Harrison, died. He was placed in a metal coffin and encased in cemented marble slabs to protect him from grave robbers.

At the funeral, members of the Harrison family noticed the grave of a friend of theirs was disturbed. The next day the Harrison family paid a surprise visit to the Ohio Medical School to see if they could locate the body of their friend. Instead, they found the corpse of John Scott Harrison. Incredibly, grave robbers had penetrated the sealed crypt of the president's father!

It did not take long for the legislature to take action. They pushed through a law making body

DIG IT

One particularly ingenious body peddler was a man named George Christian. He worked at the Surgeon General's office in Washington, D.C., and used the U.S. Army Medical Museum as a base to ship bodies all over the country!

snatching a crime and quickly provided legal sources of bodies for dissection. Slowly, other state laws also changed. Nobody knows when body snatching truly ended, but sometime in the early 1900s the last body snatcher finally hung up his shovel.

NO MORE SNATCHING

Thankfully, we no longer live (or die!) in fear of having our body dug up after we have been buried in a cemetery. But in some ways, we should be grateful for grave robbers — the service they provided for doctors helped advance medical science. The knowledge doctors have gained as a result could help to keep us *all* from early graves!

THE DEAD, THE DOOMED, AND THE BURIED:
THE ULTIMATE CHALLENGE

You've explored mummies' caves, terrifying towers, and spooky ships. You're practically an expert on the cursed and the coffined! Now test your knowledge (and don't go digging for clues in the chapters)!

1. **In the 1670s, a trunk containing human bones was found where in the Tower of London?**
   a.   in the attic
   b.   in the polar bear cage
   c.   at the foot of a staircase

2. **Which president's father's body was snatched?**
   a.   Abraham Lincoln's
   b.   Ronald Reagan's
   c.   Benjamin Harrison's

3. **White Star created their luxury ships for what types of passengers?**
   a.   rich and famous
   b.   immigrants
   c.   soldiers

4. Burying the dead in churches became a problem because:

    a.   there was no room on the pews for the parishioners

    b.   the decomposing bodies made the churches smell bad

    c.   it was too difficult to transport the bodies to the church

5. During the Civil War, Dr. Thomas Holmes preserved soldiers' bodies with:

    a.   arsenic

    b.   tomato juice

    c.   formaldehyde

6. The Chachapoya were primarily killed off by:

    a.   wild animals

    b.   European diseases

    c.   a body snatcher

7. How long did it take the *Britannic* to sink?

    a.   less than three hours

    b.   fifty-five minutes

    c.   five minutes

8. In 1066, the English Saxons were defeated by:

    a.   Swedes

    b.   Normans

    c.   Spanish invaders

9. The Chachapoya wrapped their dead in:

    a.   handmade textiles

    b.   wild grasses

    c.   toilet paper

10. The first body snatchers were:

    a.   condemned murderers

    b.   small-time crooks

    c.   medical instructors

ANSWERS TO
THE DEAD, THE DOOMED, AND THE BURIED:
THE ULTIMATE CHALLENGE

1. c	2. c
3. a	4. b
5. a	6. b
7. b	8. b
9. a	10. c

Scorecard:

If you answered **more than 7** questions correctly, congrats: You are a certified expert on all matters dead, doomed, and buried! When it comes to mummies, crypts, or sinking ships, there's no fooling you.

If you answered **more than 5** questions correctly, you've sure got a good feel for history's creepy side.

If you answered **4 or fewer** questions correctly, you may need to sharpen your sense of doom! Check back in the chapters and see if you can dig up the right answers on your own!

GLOSSARY

ANESTHESIA (an-uh-THEEZ-ya): complete or partial loss of sensation.

ARMORY (AHR-muhr-ee): a storehouse for weapons.

BULKHEAD (buhlk-HEHD): a partition or wall separating compartments in a ship.

CADAVER (cuh-DA-ver): a dead body, corpse.

CREMATION (kree-MAY-shun): the incineration or burning of a corpse.

EMBALM (ehm-BAHLM): to treat a corpse with preservatives to prevent decay.

FORMALDEHYDE (four-MAL-duh-hide): a colorless, gaseous compound used in water as a preservative and disinfectant.

GARRISON (GAIR-uhs-un): a military installation.

GENTEEL (jen-TEEL): refined, polite.

GIBBET (JIB-uht): a framework from which criminals are hanged: gallows.

MINT: a place where coins are manufactured.

MOORINGS: stabilizing lines, cables, or anchors used to secure ships and other craft.

MORGUE (MORG): a place where the bodies of the dead are kept until identified and/or claimed.

PICTOGRAPH (PIK-tuh-graf): an ancient or prehistoric drawing or painting on a rock wall.

PYRE (PIE-ER): a pile of flammable material used for burning a corpse as a funeral rite.

SHAMAN (SHAH-muhn): a priest or medicine man who uses magic to foretell events and cure the sick.

TREASON (TREE-zuhn): the betrayal of one's own country especially by acting to aid its enemies during war.

WINCH: a tool for pulling, consisting of a rope that is attached to the load and wound up as the load is pulled (used as part of a torture device in the Tower of London).

HISTORY HAS NEVER BEEN SO MUCH FUN!

Other books in THE HISTORY CHANNEL® PRESENTS Series that you will enjoy:

THE HISTORY CHANNEL® PRESENTS THE REAL SCORPION KING

You've heard about the incredible legend. But did you know that the Scorpion King was a real person who lived and ruled in ancient Egypt? Join us on a thrilling adventure as we travel back in time to a land of mummies, pharaohs, and pyramids. We'll investigate age-old mysteries and get up close and personal with some creepy desert scorpions. We're on a quest to discover the truth about a powerful ruler who may have changed civilization. Get ready to meet the amazing King Scorpion!

THE HISTORY CHANNEL® PRESENTS HISTORY UNDERCOVER®: TOP SECRET

Want to hear a secret? Come along and investigate the world's most confidential cases ever. You'll meet spies who can read minds, members of a mysterious club, and daring heroes who can change the course of history. You'll travel through time and across the globe in search of secrets so incredible . . . you may have trouble keeping them to yourself!

THE HISTORY CHANNEL® PRESENTS HISTORY'S MYSTERIES®: BIZARRE BEINGS

What are mummies made of? Are alien bodies hidden somewhere on Earth? What does the Loch Ness monster eat for breakfast? You'll find answers to these questions—and much, much more—in this chronicle of the world's creepiest creatures.